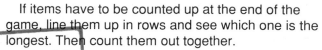
Another basic concept that children need to grasp is that the number of objects in a group does not change when they are arranged in different ways. This is known as "conservation of number" and your child can be introduced to this by playing Count the spots on page 6 and Jungle safari on page 22. Knowing where a number comes in relation to other numbers is also a useful skill and children can have a practice at this in Spiders go home on page 16 and also in Cups and saucers on page 12.

Becoming familiar with ordinal numbers, first, second, third and so on, enables children to know where things come in order. By racing teddy bears (page18) children will have a good introduction to these numbers.

Making the games

Before you start some of the games, you will need to make a few items. This is a valuable activity in itself and will afford opportunities for talking about numbers.

If your child's pencil control is fairly good, you could draw any numbers needed in pencil, for your child to trace over in felt-tip pen. This is good practice for learning to write numbers at a later stage.

Allow your child to help you use a ruler when you are measuring. Explain what you are doing and let her try to find the numbers you need and mark the right place with a pencil.

Playing the games

Most of the games are played on the opened pages of the book, using dice, counters or cards. While playing the games, encourage your child to do your counting as well as her own. Count out loud together slowly and deliberately.

If items have to be counted up at the end of the game, line them up in rows and see which one is the longest. Then count them out together.

When using plastic numbers, it is a good idea to place them on a piece of plain paper where they can be clearly seen, and will relate more easily to a written number.

If your child finds it difficult to pick up a single card from a pile, spread them out face down on the floor instead, to be picked up at random.

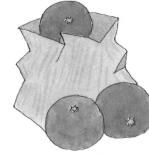

Give children all the help and support they need to create a relaxed atmosphere.

Having fun

You can work through this book from beginning to end or dip into it at random, bearing in mind that the simpler games come at the beginning. However you choose to use it, the emphasis should always be on having fun. If your child finds a game which she enjoys and wants to play again and again, she will be reinforcing the skills she has acquired. If she becomes bored or tired before a game is finished, stop the game or change the activity to shorten it.

Children learn at very different rates and have different attention spans. The most effective way to help your child is to be guided by her natural attention span and to recognize her individual learning pace.

 6 7 8 9 10

3

Candles on the cake

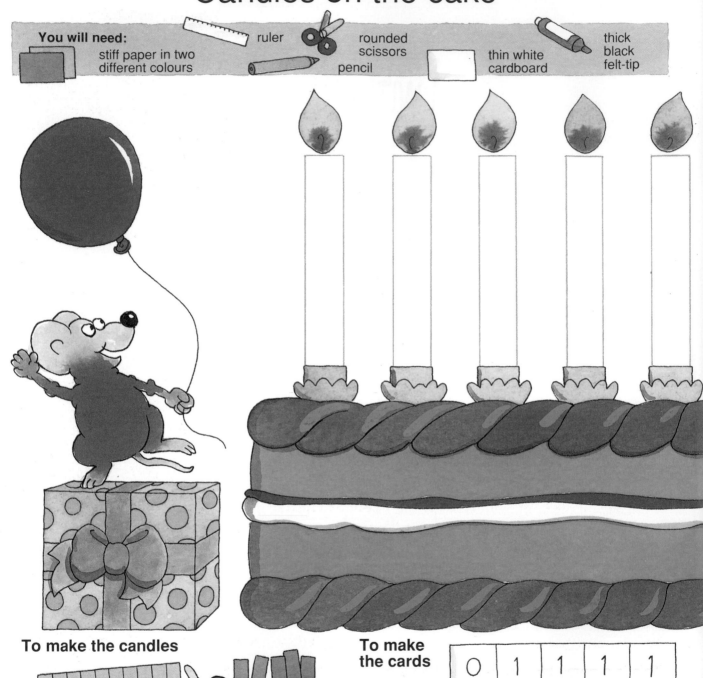

You will need:
stiff paper in two different colours
ruler
rounded scissors
pencil
thin white cardboard
thick black felt-tip

To make the candles

Cut the paper into pieces 10cm by 5½cm (4in by 2in). Using a pencil and ruler, divide the pieces into strips 5½cm (2in) long and 1cm (½in) wide. Now cut them into "candles".

To make the cards

Copy the numbers shown here.

O	1	1	1	1
O	2	2	2	2

Cut a piece of thin white cardboard to measure 20cm by 10cm (8in by 4in). Then using a pencil and ruler, divide it into ten rectangles. Clearly mark the numbers with felt-tip pen in the spaces and then cut along the lines to make ten cards.

To play the game

This is a game for two. Shuffle the cards and place them face down. Each player, in turn, takes a card and puts candles on the cake above, according to the number marked - "0","1" or "2". You must have an exact number to fill the last spaces.

The game is over when all the spaces for the candles have been filled. Take off all the candles and lay them in two lines according to colour. Whoever has the longest row is the winner.

5

Count the spots

You will need:
plastic counters
1 colour per player
(you can use squares of thin cardboard)

thick black
felt-tip pen

rounded
scissors

ruler

thin
white cardboard

To make the cards

4cm
(1½in)

5cm
(2in)

| 1 | 2 |
| 3 | 4 |

Cut thin white cardboard
into pieces 4cm by 5cm
(1½in by 2in).

Write "1" on three cards, "2"
on three cards, "3" on three
cards and "4" on the rest.

To play the game

This is for two to three players. Each player has 10 counters.

Shuffle the cards and place them face down between the players. The players take turns in taking a card and then, according to the number shown, putting a counter on the creature or flower with the same number of spots. Cards are put back under the pile. If a player cannot find a number to match, she misses a turn.

The game ends when all the creatures and flowers on the page are "claimed". Add the counters to find the winner.

Another idea

Later on, you could make cards with spots grouped in different patterns to be matched with the spots on the page.

Win a prize

You will need: set of plastic numbers (you can use magnetic numbers) paper bag plastic or paper counters in two different colours

8

To play the game

This is a game for two players.

Put the plastic numbers into a bag. The players take turns to pick out a number and see if they can match it to one on the picture. If they can, a counter is put on the object they have won. The numbers are returned to the bag. The game finishes when all the "prizes" have been won.

Collect the counters and count them up to see who has the most. You could also lay them in two rows according to their colour and see who has the longest line.

9

Pie in the oven

You will need: 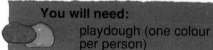 playdough (one colour per person) one screw-on bottle top per person dice egg cup for dice

3 Go on 2

4

5

Bird pecks pie Go back 3  **13**

14

2

6 Greedy cat  Go back to start

12

1

7

11

Start

8 Spilled milk Go back 1

Go on 2 **9**

10

To make the pies

Roll a small piece of playdough into a ball and press it inside a bottle top. Place a tiny ball of playdough on top.

Mark a pattern around the edge using the end of a plastic straw. Make a pie for each player using a different colour.

Hints

- If you have only one colour playdough, make different markings on the pies, or colour them with some food colouring.

- Use large buttons if you don't want to make pies.

10

plastic straw

Lose rolling pin
Miss a turn

15

16

17

18

19

Have another turn

21
Oven too hot
Go back 2

20
Hungry mouse
Go back 1

22

23

Finish

To play the game

Place your pies on the table marked "Start". The first player rolls the dice and moves his pie along the number of places shown by the dice. He can count aloud as he goes. He must then follow any instructions on the square where he lands. The next player then has a turn. Whoever gets his pie in the oven first is the winner. An exact number on the dice must be rolled to finish.

Learning notes

While playing this game your child will start recognizing numbers from the dot patterns on dice. Counting out skills are also required here. This will help your child to see the sequence of numbers.

11

Cups and saucers

 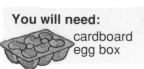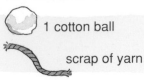
To make the cups

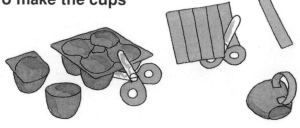

To make the mouse

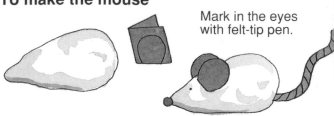

Mark in the eyes with felt-tip pen.

Cut the egg box into six separate sections and trim around each edge to make six cup shapes.

Cut six strips of stiff paper 5cm by 1cm (2in by ½in). Glue one end near the top of the cup and then bend the strip back and glue it at the base.

Pull off one third of a cotton ball and then tease it into a pear shape.

Cut out pink paper ears and glue them onto the head end. Stick on a tiny paper nose and a scrap of yarn for the tail.

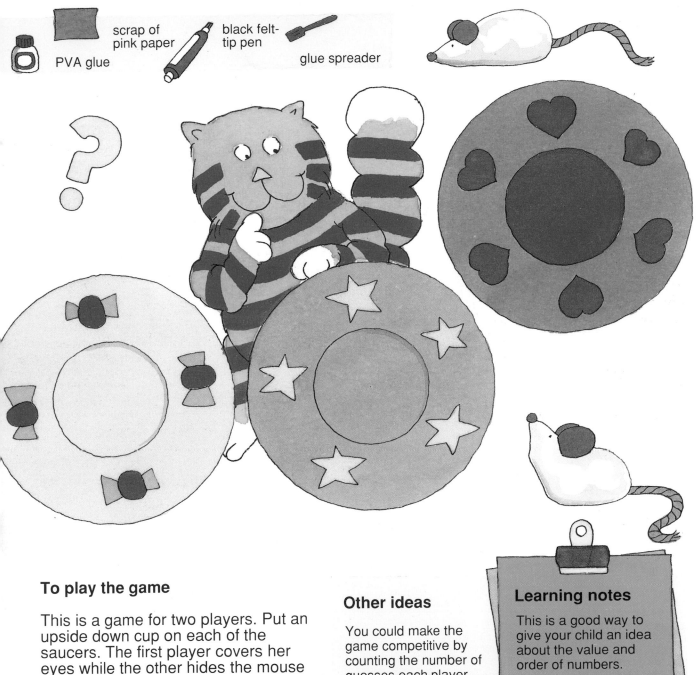

scrap of
pink paper

black felt-
tip pen

PVA glue

glue spreader

To play the game

This is a game for two players. Put an upside down cup on each of the saucers. The first player covers her eyes while the other hides the mouse under a cup. The first player then has to guess where the mouse is hiding, while the second player gives clues.

For example, if the mouse is under the number "5" a guess of "2" would mean the second player would say "higher"; if the guess is "6" she would say "lower", and so on until the mouse is found. Players take turns guessing and hiding.

Other ideas

You could make the game competitive by counting the number of guesses each player takes to find a mouse.

If you don't want to make cups, use yogurt pots or something similar. You can use a large button instead of a mouse.

Learning notes

This is a good way to give your child an idea about the value and order of numbers.

Build a house bingo

You will need: ruler, pencil

thin red cardboard, set of plastic numbers, rounded scissors, paper bag

1		
7	4	
6	8	5
9	4	8
3	6	2
7	5	9

To make the bricks

6cm (2½in)

Cut a piece of thin red cardboard to measure 30cm by 6cm (12in by 2½in). With a pencil, rule it into 30 rectangles, each 3cm wide and 2cm long (1¼in by ¾in). Cut them out to make bricks.

14

To play the game

This is a game for 2 players. Each player has 15 red bricks. Players choose which house on the double page they would like to build. Put the plastic numbers in the bag.

Players then take turns pulling a number out of the bag. (They mustn't look.) If a player picks a number which matches the number on a brick space on her house, she can cover the space with a red brick. The number is put back into the bag - give the bag a shake between turns. The first player to build her house (that is, cover the brick spaces) is the winner.

15

Spiders go home

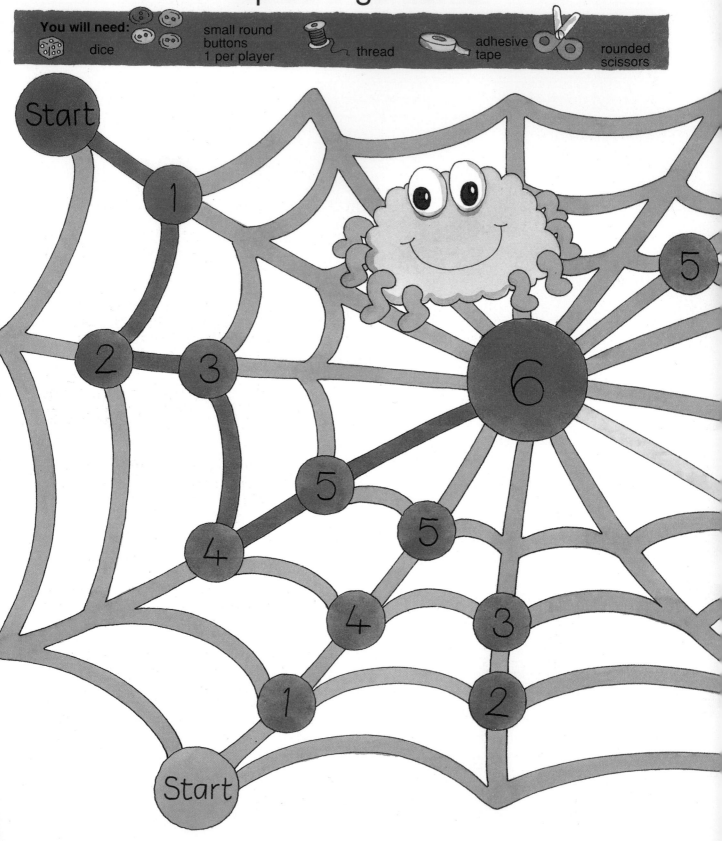

You will need: dice — small round buttons 1 per player — thread — adhesive tape — rounded scissors

16

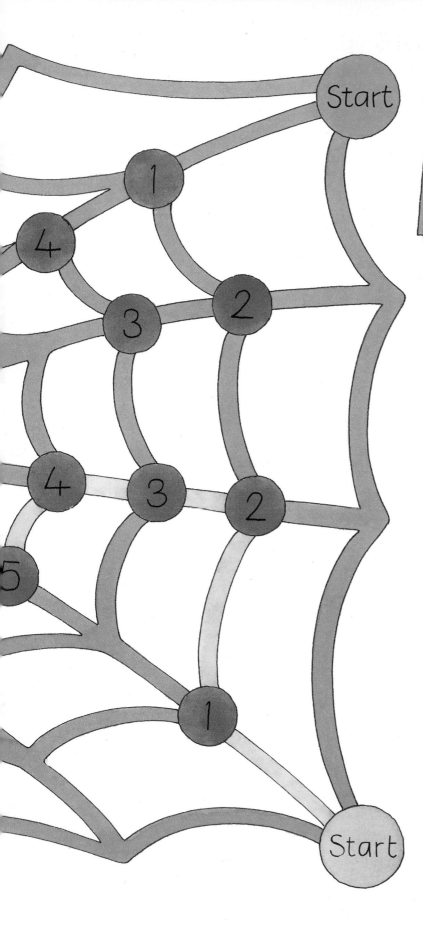

To make the baby spiders

Cut a small piece of tape and then lay four lengths of thread on the sticky side. Now press on a small round button.

The holes in the buttons are the eyes.

Trim the legs so they are about 1cm (½in) each side. Make one spider for each player.

To play the game

This game is for two or three players.

Each player chooses a path on the spider's web and places a baby spider on a "Start" place. The players take turns throwing the dice. In order to move to the first position players must throw a "1". To move to the next place on the web they must throw a "2" and so on until a "6" is thrown and a baby spider reaches home. The first player to do this is the winner.

Once children get the idea of this game they can play it by themselves, racing one spider against another.

Teddy bear race

You will need:
One teddy bear per player

rounded scissors

dinner plate

old newspaper

To make a spinner

With a piece of chalk, draw around a dinner plate on some hard flat ground. If you are indoors, draw on a piece of cardboard.

Mark six sections on the circle, as shown. Number each section from 1-6. Put the plastic knife in the middle.

To make a path

Cut newspaper into rectangles that are large enough for teddies to sit on. Lay two winding paths across the floor or garden using an equal number of sheets - 15 or more.

18

chalk

plastic knife

If it is a windy day, weigh the paper down with stones.

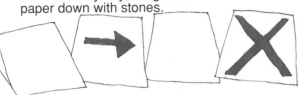

You can mark a large cross on the "start", and "finish" squares, and draw arrows along the path.

To play the game

This is a game for two players.

Players take turns to spin the knife and see which number the blade end points to. They then move their teddy that number of squares along their chosen path. The first teddy to reach the end of the path wins - an exact number must be spun in order to reach the end of the path.

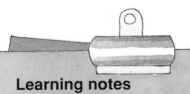

Learning notes

This active counting-out game will introduce such ordinal numbers as "first" and "second". Your child can eventually play this game himself, racing toys against each other.

Outdoor counting games

Throw and count

Players take turns throwing balls into a large cardboard box with a hole cut in its side. The balls can be made from rolled up socks. Players have six turns. Use a piece of string as a starting line. Count up the "hits" and "misses".

Find and count

Give each player a sheet of paper with numbers 1-6 written on it – space out the numbers well. Players look around the garden and collect objects to match the numbers on their sheet. They can find leaves, twigs, fallen petals and so on. Make sure they know that such objects as flower heads are not to be collected.

Spotting game

Set tasks for your child when out on a journey. Ask her to spot 2 horses, 10 red cars, 3 white trucks and so on.

New shoes

To make the spinner

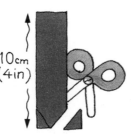

Turn over a large paper plate and on the back rule it into four sections. Number the sections as shown.

Cut a piece of thin cardboard into a strip 10cm by 2cm (4in by ¾in). Snip one end of the strip to make a point.

Poke a hole in the middle of the plate and in the pointer 1cm (½in) from its straight edge. Use a ballpoint pen to do this.

thick black
felt-tip
pen

2 small bowls

thin
cardboard

Widen holes if the pointer does not spin.

1 2 3

Push a paper fastener through the pointer and the middle of the plate, and then open its wings. Make sure the pointer spins smoothly.

To play the game

This game is for two players. The idea of the game is to fit on the caterpillar's new "pairs" of shoes.

Put a pile of pasta shells between the players, and give them a bowl each. Players take turns spinning the pointer. They then take the number of pasta shells shown by the pointer and place the "pasta" shoes, in pairs, on the caterpillar's feet. Any odd shoes left over are kept in the players' bowls to be counted later. For instance, a "4" turned up means two pairs of shoes can be fitted; a three will mean one pair plus an odd one left over.

When the caterpillar has all his shoes fitted, players count up the number of "odd" shoes they have each collected in their bowls. Whoever has the smallest number of "odd" shoes is the winner.

21

Jungle safari

You will need:
thin white cardboard · thick black felt-tip pen · pencil · ruler · rounded scissors · paper in two different colours

To make the cards

Cut thin white cardboard into 8 pieces measuring 5cm by 4cm (3in by 1½in). Now number the cards, as shown, draw a bush on one of the remaining cards and a raincloud on the other.

To make the tents

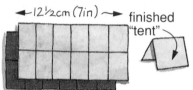

12½cm (7in) → finished "tent"

Cut the paper into pieces measuring 12½cm by 6cm (7in by 2½in). Now draw ten rectangles on each piece measuring 3cm by 2½cm (1¼in by ¾in) and cut them out. Fold them by putting the short edges together, then open them slightly so they stand like tents.

To play the game

This is a game for two players. The object of the game is to see who can "spot" the most animals - to do this players have to set up their tents in the jungle.

Each player chooses a tent colour. Shuffle the cards together and place them face down between the players. Players take turns picking up a card and reading the number. If the number on the card can be matched to a group of animals, for example, a "2" card is matched to two lions, then the lions are claimed by a player pitching his tent by them. If a number can't be matched a turn is missed.

If a bush is turned up, it means the animals are hiding and no tents can be placed. If a player picks a raincloud, one of his tents has been washed away and he must take it away.

When all the cards are used, they are re-shuffled and play begins again. The game is over when all the animals have a tent pitched by them. The winner has the most tents set up.

Rabbit tails

You will need:

PVA glue — glue spreader — pink and white cotton balls — stiff white paper — thin white cardboard — rounded scissors — felt-tip pens

To make the rabbit tails

Cut two pieces of stiff white paper 5cm by 4cm (2in by 1½in). Cover them with glue then spread and press a white cotton ball on one piece, and a pink cotton ball on the other.

Let the glue dry thoroughly. Now cut the pieces into small squares about 1cm by 1cm (½in by ½in). These are your rabbit tails.

To make the cards

Cut thin white cardboard into 12 pieces 5cm by 4cm (2in by 1½in). Draw large carrots on two of the cards; write "1" on four cards; "2" on three cards; "3" on two cards and "4" on the remaining one.

24

To play the game

This is a game for two players. Players choose pink or white tails. The cards are shuffled and placed face down in a pile. Players take turns picking up a card and, according to the number shown, putting tails on the rabbits. For instance, if a "3" card is turned up, three of the rabbits on the page can be given a tail.

If a carrot card is turned up, two tails have to be taken away. The game is over when all the rabbits have tails - an exact number has to be turned up to finish. Take off the tails and lay them in two rows by colour. The longest row is the winner.

Other ideas

Start with an equal number of tails on the page, and then take them off according to the number shown on the cards. A carrot card means you must put back two tails. The first one to remove all her tails is the winner.

For very young children, you could use this picture to play counting games. For example, see how many white rabbits there are, or how many are eating, jumping, hiding, have floppy ears and so on.

25

Cherry pie

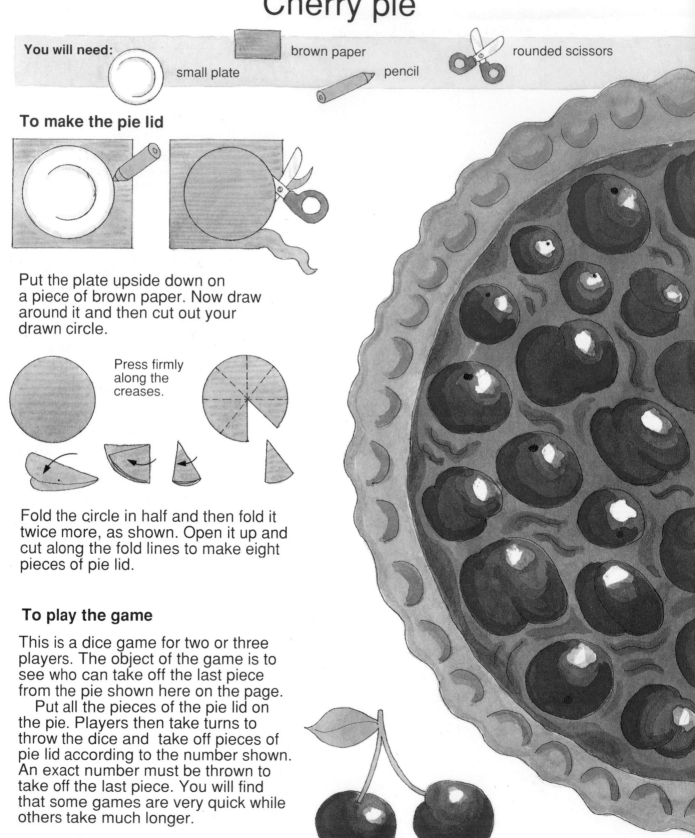

You will need: small plate, brown paper, pencil, rounded scissors

To make the pie lid

Put the plate upside down on a piece of brown paper. Now draw around it and then cut out your drawn circle.

Press firmly along the creases.

Fold the circle in half and then fold it twice more, as shown. Open it up and cut along the fold lines to make eight pieces of pie lid.

To play the game

This is a dice game for two or three players. The object of the game is to see who can take off the last piece from the pie shown here on the page.

Put all the pieces of the pie lid on the pie. Players then take turns to throw the dice and take off pieces of pie lid according to the number shown. An exact number must be thrown to take off the last piece. You will find that some games are very quick while others take much longer.

26

dice

Learning notes

This is a good game to start children predicting numbers. Try to encourage them to figure out what number they need to roll in order to win the game. The game also introduces the idea of "taking away" as pieces are removed and the rest are counted.

Other ideas

Players could keep a game score by collecting a "cherry stone" - a small prize - each time they win a game. After an agreed number of games, say, five, the "cherry stones" are counted up and whoever has the most is the winner.

Try playing this game the other way around and put the pieces on the pie according to the numbers on the dice.

27

Park your cars

You will need:

thin white
cardboard

ruler

rounded
scissors

felt-tip
pens

CARS

LIFT 10	LIFT 10
9	9
8	8
7	7
START 6	START 6
5	5

To make the cards

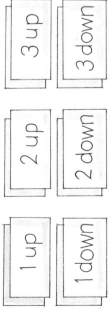

From thin white cardboard cut 12 cards measuring 5cm by 4cm (2in by 1½in). Mark the cards as shown (two of each).

Make four more cards to measure 4½cm by 2cm (1¾in by ¾in). Then draw a truck, a car, or a van on each of these smaller cards.

To play the game

This is a game for two players. Each has two "car" cards. Players choose the red or blue car lift. They then put one of their cars on "floor 6".

The large cards are shuffled and then placed face down in a pile. Players take turns picking a card and moving their vehicles up or down according to the instructions on the card. If a car lands next to an empty parking space it can be moved into that space, only then can a player put his second car on the "Start" position. If a card shows a greater number than there are spaces to move, the player has to miss a turn. The first person to park both his vehicles is the winner.

Learning notes

In this game, your child will be counting on and back along a line so introducing, in a very practical way, first elements of adding and subtracting.

Hint

You can use tiny toy cars instead of "car" cards.

31

Materials and equipment

Some of the games in this book involve making things as well as playing, and it can be fun for you and your child to cut, paint and glue together. You can store your game pieces in envelopes and cover any cards with sticky-backed plastic for safe-keeping.

The specific things you need for each project are listed at the top of each page. Below is some general advice on materials and equipment.

Plastic numbers are often magnetic and can be bought in educational toy stores. You can always use small cards with numbers written on if you don't own a set.

Scissors should be rounded . If you use sharp scissors don't forget to put them away after use. Try and draw clear outlines for your child to cut. If you are cutting out cards or paper "bricks", it is a good idea to cut long strips and then let your child cut them up into smaller separate pieces.

Felt-tip pens should be non-toxic and washable. Use thick or thin ones depending on the size of paper you are using. Black numbers written on white is very clear and easily understood.

Glue: PVA glue (polyvinyl acetate) is a safe glue for your child to use. You can buy it in large stationery stores or educational toy stores. It is washable, but it is a good idea to wipe up spills as soon as possible and to wear aprons or overalls. If it is spilled on clothes, soak them in cold water to make sure there is no staining. PVA can also be used as a paint thickener or varnish: it is white but is clear when dry. Glue sticks are good for using on small areas.

When gluing small pieces, such as wool tails on mice, it is a good idea to pour a little glue into an old saucer and lightly dip in the pieces rather than use a glue brush.

Thin cardboard can be bought in art supply stores and stationery stores. Stiff, thick paper is a good alternative, but make sure that the numbers can't be seen when the cards are face down.

Coloured papers can be saved from used packaging. Unused wallpapers will give you different colours and patterns when you need a contrast. You can also colour stiff white paper with paint mixed with a little PVA glue.

Paints should be water-based and non-toxic. Mix or thin colours on old plates, and use mugs for water as they are safer than glass containers.

Playdough is available from toy and stationery stores. You can also use a little uncooked pastry dyed with a little food colouring, or mix flour, salt and water to a playdough texture.

Bags: it is a good idea, when using bags for a game, to remind children never to put any kind of bag over their heads.